Zodiac Knights 2000 Featuring Creatures of the Knights

Creatures of the Knights (A New Era)

By

Isaac A. Potter Jr./Samuel J. Potter

ISBN: 1-4107-2460-3 (e-book)
ISBN: 1-4107-2461-1 (Paperback)

This book is printed on acid free paper.

Illustrations by Isaac A. Potter Jr.
Agent – Shannon M. Fridel

Library of Congress Control Number: 2003092487

Printed in the United States of America
Bloomington, IN

1st Books - rev. 4/21/03

Special fighting power: Battering ram head, ram fist
Weapon: Ram spear, ram head
Transport: Ram staff transport
Location: Rome

Aquarius: Water Wizard
Special fighting power: controls and alters liquid
Transport: Aqua staff transport
Location: Hawaii

Cancer: Wrestler
Special fighting power: crippling claw
Weapon: flying claw stars
Transport: Cancer staff transport
Location: Germany

Capricorn: Ancient fighter
Special fighting power: Ninja swordsman
Weapon: swords, daggers
Transport: unicorn staff transport
Location: Japan

Gemini: Multiple twin fighters
Special fighting power: Merges into twin fighters during battle
Weapon: Twin hand blades
Transport: Twin staff transport
Location: Hong Kong

Leo: Computer scientist
Special fighting power: Z-claws
Weapon: Z-claws, shattering roars
Transport: lion staff
Location: Africa

Libra: Wise man
Special fighting power: Kick boxer
Weapon: Spinning scales
Transport: Scale of balance staff
Location: Russia

Pisces: Olympia swimmer
Special fighting power: Fist of Fins
Weapon: Fist of fins, head fins
Transport: Sting ray staff
Location: Alaska

Sagittarius: Archery expert
Special fighting power: Speed, Strength, and stamina
Weapon: Bows and Spears
Transport: Stallion staff
Location: America

Scorpio: Dessert Hunter
Special fighting Power: Jujitsu Master
Weapon: Laser tail, paralyzing stinger
Transport: scorpion staff
Location: Jamaica

Taurus: Power lifter
Special fighting power: brut strength
Weapon: Brut strength, bull club, bullwhip
Transport: Bull staff
Location: Mexico

Virgo: Sorceress
Special fighting power: Karate
Weapon: Medieval sorcery
Transport: crystal staff
Location: Bermuda

This first short story is dedicated in memory of our Great Grandmother, Pattie Mae Sampson, Sister, Patricia R. Potter, Samantha Potter (Cherry), Johnny Potter Sr., Uncle Bubba (Johnny Potter Jr.), and our living parents Isaac and Thelma Potter.

THE ZODIAC KNIGHTS 2000

In the beginning, Merlin was the greatest wizard known to the medieval era; but even the greatest of wizards can have a bad day. A day of havoc for a wizard can sometimes be beneficial to the future of mankind in a mystical kind of way. A mystical spell performed incorrectly could bring forth cause and effect to its past, present, and future existence. Because Merlin was well known and basically dominated the Circle of Magic; one could only expect there would be some sort of envious evil lurking around every dark cold corner. An evil mortal being, the servant of Merlin's, felt that if was unfair for an immortal such as Merlin to receive all the fame and glory upon his expense of contributing to Merlin's success. The day would come when the servant would no longer want to serve as an understudy for Merlin and he would have his time of reckoning and the world would know of his true identity; along with the skills and powers that earned great success for Merlin.

The evil servant set forth to ruin Merlin's name as well as his reputation with the people of all the villages on the exact day and time that Merlin would perform his annual Spell of Harvest for the four seasons of the year.

This spell included the arranging of Mother Natures weather patterns to benefit all the farmers and their annual crops. All the servant had to do was to mix match a few ingredients in the wrong tubes and watch Merlin finally fall deep in his own pit of failure. This would cause the people of the villages to cast him out forever into the deep dark parts of the earth, never to be heard from again.

Merlin, who was caught up in the special attention and over whelmed with his ability to win the villagers over with his magic, did indeed cast the spell and everything was going according to plan, as the evil servant had planned. Merlin was banished from the village, never to hear from again, but the spell did cause the evil servant to reap his faith in return. The chemicals exploded directly in the face of the evil servant causing him to mutate into something grotesque. Poof! The evil servant is no longer, but he now proclaimed himself the Insect Warlord.

Merlin failed with dismay and immediately disappeared and was never heard from again, but on the other hand the spell also caused a metabolic change in several other creatures that was caught in the path of the spell. The fumes from the spell ascended into the laboratory and out into the heavens and the Earth mutating creatures into what is now known as the "ZODIAC KNIGHTS 2000". After the tremendous explosion and the poisonous fumes cleared, the small laboratory of Merlin the Evil Servant rose from the ashes with his new found hideous appearance, laughing and proclaiming himself a new breed of Warlock.

The insect in the laboratory that mutated into hideous creatures quickly became known as "The Insect Warlords" servants, for he created the spell which gave him control over the who is now the Insect Warriors. The Evil Insect Warlord sent forth the Insect Warriors to do his evil biding and destroy anything and anyone in his path in order to take over the Earth and the entire Universe, for that matter.

Insect Warlord did not know that the spell also created the Zodiac Knights 2000, whose duty was to protect and preserve mankind and life, as it is known at its present time. Each Zodiac Knight would acquire his or her own special skills and abilities to aid them in time of need, for they were now the guardians of the Earth and all her treasures. In the meantime the Zodiac Knights roamed the Earth not in total control of their skills and their mission, the creatures eventually crossed each other's paths and bonded together in their travels across the Earth. The Knights skills were well below par, along with their experience and knowledge in which they would need in time of battle. Help was only several centuries away and it had to be a blood relative of Merlin.

In the meantime, the evil warlord had heard rumors of these freaks created from his blunder of a spell. Which he had involuntarily created in his attempt to ruin Merlin, which brought forth a solution to benefit mankind and creates a balance in his rise to a wicked fame and glory. The evil warlord plotted to trap and defuse the Earth's only protectors that could cause him any problems now or in the near future. A problem that caused the first problem would be his solution to solving his present problem; the evil warlord would create a volcanic eruption and bury the insect warriors along with the zodiac knights, during the heat of a premeditated battle, only he would create. The Insect Warlord thought that he would be the only one able to resurrect the creatures that held him from his fame and glory, little did he know that it would take only a blood relative of Merlin to open the tomb. Sir Isaac and Lord Abraham would be those non-suspecting relatives of Merlin that would help save mankind from destruction.

Sir Isaac is a computer wizard and has a huge appetite for snacks; Lord Abraham is known as a "Jack of all Trades." Centuries have now passed and the time has come for the awakening of the "Zodiac Knights 2000." Sir Isaac and Lord Abraham set out on a camping trip and unfortunately Lord Abraham misread the map, leading the two inexperienced explorers into an uncharted place not on the mountain map. The sun began to set which left them no choice but to set up camp and continue on the lost expedition at the break of dawn. While Sir Isaac lay asleep, a vision of a ghostly nature appeared to him; but he felt as if he had eaten too much beef stew the night before. He told Lord Abraham of this vision, and he too agreed that it could have been caused from over indulging the night before. The two explorers gathered all their camping gear and tossed a coin into the air to determine in which direction they were to travel, but leave it to lady luck, the coin landed directed into the crack of two rocks which brought them to the only conclusion available, traveling northward up the trail. As the blazing sun rose high above the mystic volcano, Sir Isaac became exhausted and sweaty, so he searched for a nice cool shaded area. Sir Isaac lay his exhausted body next to a huge bolder and drank some of the cool water from his canteen. Sir Isaac was unaware that he was a descendent of Merlin and therefore, the large bolder slowly begins to open and a musty air centuries old burst from within the tomb. Sir Isaac and Lord Abraham were overwhelmed with curiosity and they slowly entered the tomb, not knowing what they were about to encounter. One must remember that the Zodiac Knights and the Insect Warriors were placed under the same spell and buried in the same location for centuries; If Sir Isaac accidentally awaken the wrong creatures, it could create all types of havoc. Merlin's spirit tried to make contact with Sir Isaac the night before, but the spirit failed in it's attempt to communicate because Sir Isaac's electronic gadgets placed an electronic field around his body. Sir Isaac had no clue of who was who or which was which, sure! Sir Isaac touched the wrong creatures tomb embedded in lava the "The Insect

Warriors." The cavern begun to shake violently and rocks began to fall from every angle. Sir Isaac and Lord Abraham quickly ran out of the cavern and down into the lower valley. The two explorers sat in fear, watching the entrance to see what was about to burst from within the cavern, used as a tomb for many centuries, which they had unleashed. Behold! The Insect Warriors were finally free to complete their mission they had been given centuries ago; the mission was to destroy the Zodiac Knights and bring mankind to its knees. Would Sir Isaac and Lord Abraham gather up enough courage to awaken the Guardians of Mother Earth?

ZODIAC
KNIGHTS 2000
Hear No Evil

```
NAME: JR.

HEIGHT:  3'

     35#

SPECIAL FIGHTING POWERS:   TUCK AND ROLL, MUNCH BOX
                           ATTACK
```

JR., IKE's GRANDSON, HAS A TREMENDOUS APPETITE
FOR SNACKS, COMPUTER WHIZ, AND ALSO A VIDEO GAME
MANIAC. JR.'s TOOL BOX IS FULL OF MYSTICAL
TREATS AND WHATEVER IS PULL FROM IT's CONTENTS.

NAME: IKE

HEIGHT: 5'8"

WEIGHT: 200#

SPECIAL FIGHTING POWERS: THE OLD SCHOOL SWOOP AND
                           THE CRANE UPPERCUT

JACK OF ALL TRADES, MASTER OF NONE. IKE INHERITED
A MYSTICAL TOOL BOX WHICH PROVIDED A TOOL FOR
NEARLY EVERY ADVENTURE. A PLAYBOY AT HEART.

NAME: maSKITTER

HEIGHT: 12'

WEIGHT: 400#

SPECIAL FIGHTING POWERS: INTELLIGENT-SWIFT-
AGGRESSIVE- STINGER ABSORBS FOES ENERGY.

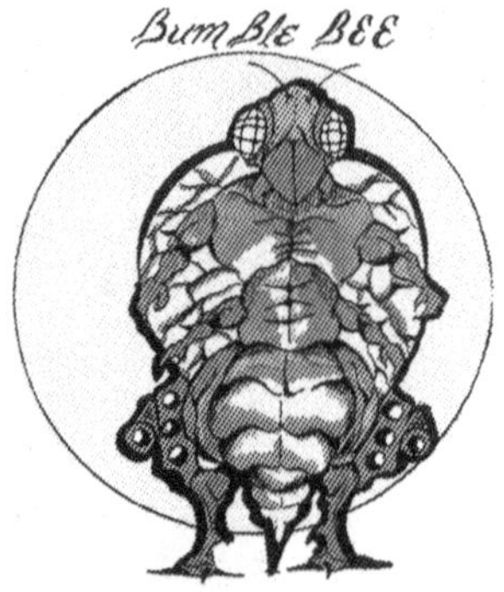

NAME: BUMBLE BEE

HEIGHT: 15'

WEIGHT: 550#

SPECIAL FIGHTING POWERS: LAZER STINGER-
THIGH SIX SHOOTER WITH HEAT SEEKING ROCKETS.

NAME: WASP

HEIGHT: 12'

WEIGHT: 475#

SPECIAL FIGHTING POWERS: TRIPLE AUTO DROP SINKER
                         C-4 STINGER

Battle Beetle
Grasshoppa
Cockaroach

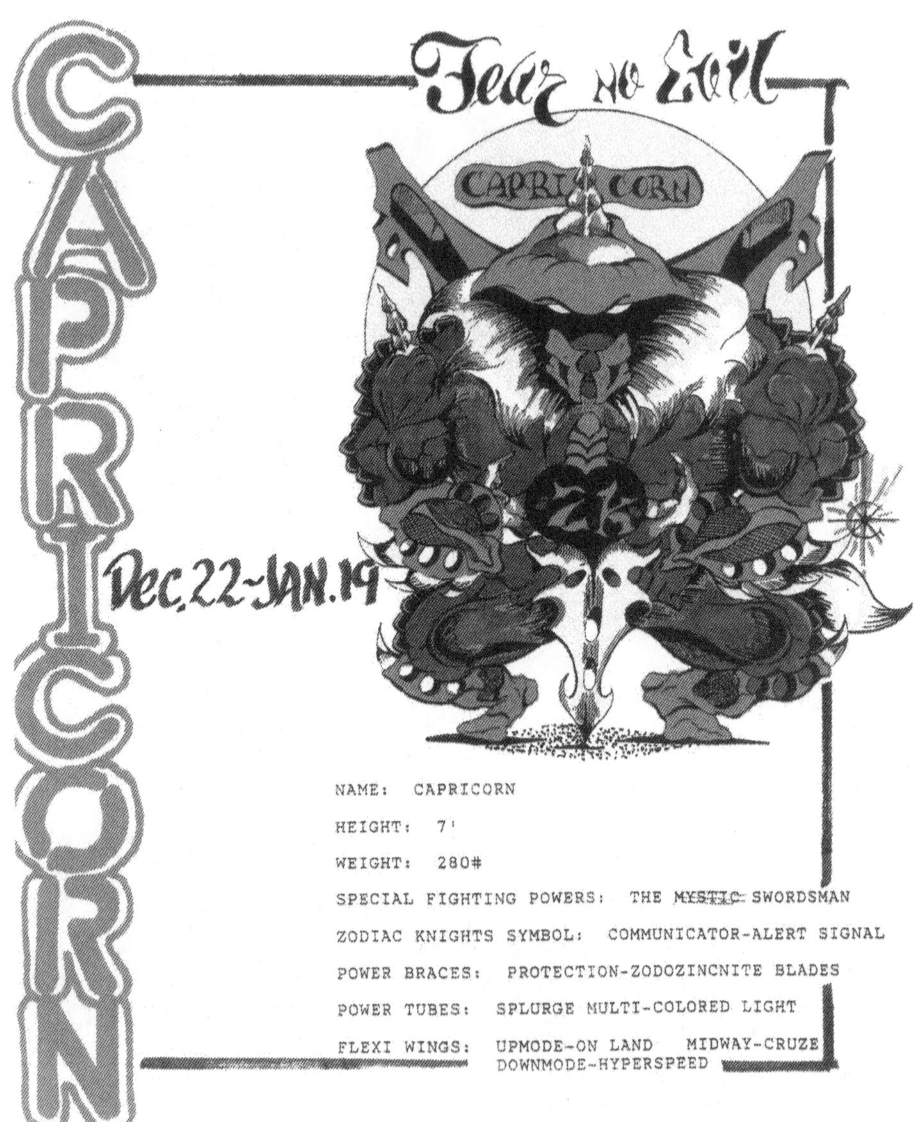

NAME: CAPRICORN

HEIGHT: 7'

WEIGHT: 280#

SPECIAL FIGHTING POWERS: THE MYSTIC SWORDSMAN

ZODIAC KNIGHTS SYMBOL: COMMUNICATOR-ALERT SIGNAL

POWER BRACES: PROTECTION-ZODOZINCNITE BLADES

POWER TUBES: SPLURGE MULTI-COLORED LIGHT

FLEXI WINGS: UPMODE-ON LAND   MIDWAY-CRUZE
DOWNMODE-HYPERSPEED

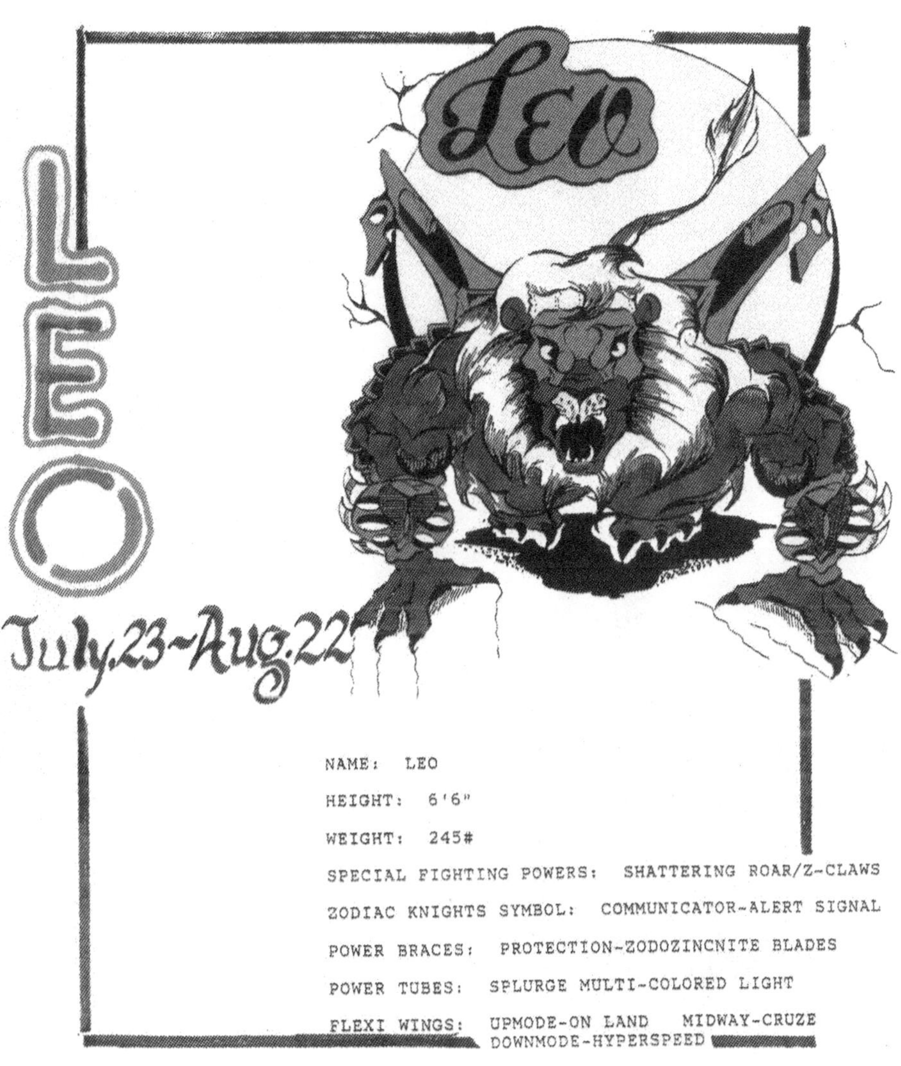


```
NAME:  LEO

HEIGHT:  6'6"

WEIGHT:  245#

SPECIAL FIGHTING POWERS:  SHATTERING ROAR/Z-CLAWS

ZODIAC KNIGHTS SYMBOL:  COMMUNICATOR-ALERT SIGNAL

POWER BRACES:  PROTECTION-ZODOZINCNITE BLADES

POWER TUBES:  SPLURGE MULTI-COLORED LIGHT

FLEXI WINGS:  UPMODE-ON LAND   MIDWAY-CRUZE
              DOWNMODE-HYPERSPEED
```

NAME: GEMINI

HEIGHT: 6'2"

WEIGHT: 220#

SPECIAL FIGHTING POWERS: KUNG-FU TWINS

ZODIAC KNIGHTS SYMBOL: COMMUNICATOR-ALERT SIGNAL

POWER BRACES: PROTECTION-ZODOZINCNITE BLADES

POWER TUBES: SPLURGE MULTI-COLORED LIGHT

FLEXI WINGS: UPMODE-ON LAND MIDWAY-CRUZE
DOWNMODE-HYPERSPEED

Pisces
Pisces

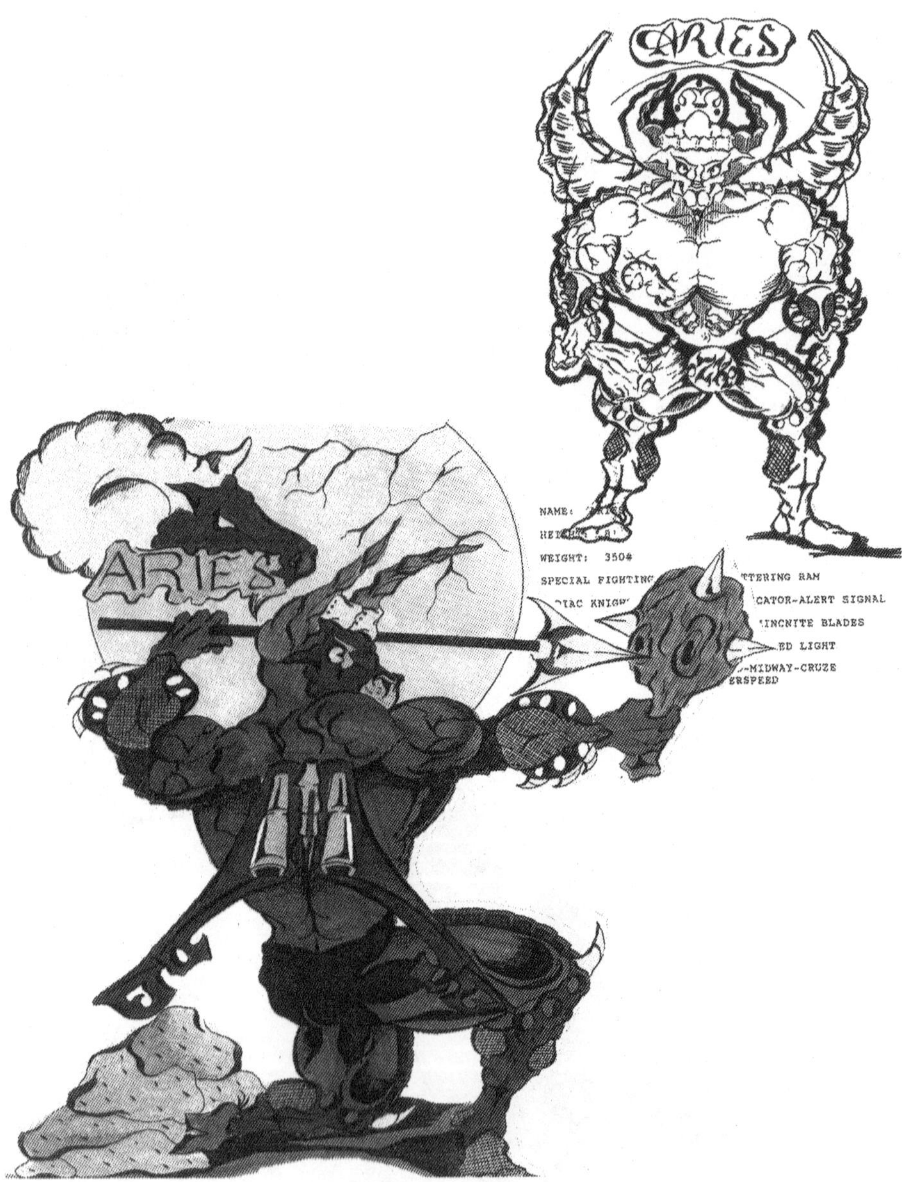
ARIES
ARIES
NAME: ARIES
HEIGHT:
WEIGHT: 350#
SPECIAL FIGHTING
TTERING RAM
DIAC KNIGH
CATOR-ALERT SIGN
INCNITE BLADES
ED LIGHT
MIDWAY-CRUZE
ERSPEED

NAME: CANCER
HEIGHT: 6'4"
WEIGHT: 280#
SPECIAL FIGHTING POWERS: THE CRIPPLING·CLAW·
ZODIAC KNIGHTS SYMBOL: COMMUNICATOR-ALERT SIGNAL
POWER BRACES: PROTECTION-ZODOZINCNITE BLADES
POWER TUBES: SPLURGE MULTI-COLORED LIGHTS
FLEXI WINGS: UPMODE-ON LAND MIDWAY-cruze
             DOWNMODE-HYPERSPEED

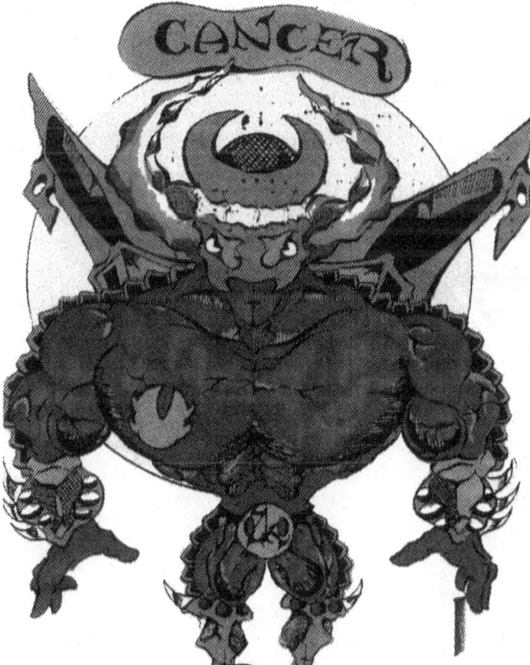

NAME: AQUARIUS

HEIGHT: 6'7"

WEIGHT: 225#

SPECIAL FIGHTING POWERS: THE WATER WIZARD

ZODIAC KNIGHTS SYMBOL: COMMUNICATOR-ALERT SIGNAL

POWER BRACES: PROTECTION-ZODOZINCNITE BLADES

POWER TUBES: SPLURGE MULTI-COLORED LIGHT

FLEXI WINGS: UPMODE-ON LAND MIDWAY-CRUZE
              DOWNMODE-HYPERSPEED

NAME: VIRGO

HEIGHT: 6'

WEIGHT: 195#

SPECIAL FIGHTING POWERS: (SORCERY)/KARATE

ZODIAC KNIGHTS SYMBOL: COMMUNICATOR-ALERT SIGNAL

POWER BRACES: PROTECTION-ZODOZINCNITE BLADES

POWER TUBES: SPLURGE MULTI-COLORED LIGHTS

FLEXI WINGS: UPMODE-ON LAND   MIDWAY-CRUZE
DOWNMODE-HYPERSPEED

TAURUS: Powerlifter
Special power: Massive Brut Strength
Zodiac symbol: communicator~ alert signal
Power Braces: Protection~zodozincnite blades
Power Tubes: Splurged Multicolored lights
FLExi Wings: upmode~onland~midway~cruze~downmode~Hyperspeed

Scorpio

NAME: SAGITTARIUS

HEIGHT: 7'

WEIGHT: 300#

SPECIAL FIGHTING POWERS: ARCHERY AND SPEAR EXPERT

ZODIAC KNIGHTS SYMBOL: COMMUNICATOR-ALERT SIGNAL

POWER BRACES: PROTECTION-ZODOZINCNITE BLADES

POWER TUBES: SPLURGE MULTI-COLORED LIGHTS

FLEXI WINGS: UPMODE-ON LAND   MIDWAY-CRUZE
              DOWNMODE-HYPERSPEED

NAME: LIBRA

HEIGHT: 6'7"

WEIGHT: 235#

SPECIAL FIGHTING POWERS: KICKBOXER-WISEMAN

ZODIAC KNIGHTS SYMBOL: COMMUNICATOR-ALERT SIGNAL

POWER BRACES: PROTECTION-ZODOZINCNITE BLADES

POWER TUBES: SPLURGE MULTI-COLORED LIGHTS

FLEXI WINGS: UPMODE-ON LAND   MIDWAY-CRUZE
DOWNMODE-HYPERSPEED

Chapter one featuring the

Creatures of the Knights

It's the year 2010; crime is at an all time high. It's no longer safe for citizens to walk the streets of America. Police have a severe shortage of manpower to control crime, as we now know it. In the mean time back in Washington, D. C., the President; of the United States has called a meeting with congress to vote on a bill that would fund a secret project to help assist in the salvation of mankind. Congress agreed to speedily past a bill that would fund a 20 million- dollar operation. The President briefed the FBI, CIA, and other special agencies on the situation at hand.

The Commander and Chief insist that the best twelve scientists around the world to placed in charge of this huge task. The FBI traced files on the twelve greatest scientific minds that were available immediately. The FBI briefed the President on a list of the most promising scientific minds available. The president gave the green light to bring the scientist back to Washington; once the scientist where in Washington D. C., they would be given a laptop computer programmed with information on the secret project.

The scientist returned to their quarters to continue their studies of the secret project; while waiting to board a plane, its destination would be to arrive in South Africa.

The scientist arrived on the out shirts of South Africa, 9:00 a.m., where they were greeted by the islanders, whom soon would become there personal escorts to the laboratory and on the project tour. The islanders unloaded the supplies and luggage that would accompany the scientist along their travel to an island called "Tobu". The research laboratory was hidden by the jungles natural habitat and only the islanders knew of its immediate location. The scientist help the islanders unload the large boat, which was also covered with natural jungle habitat. The islanders escorted the scientist eagerly to their quarters where the secret research project would begin. One of the islanders provided translation for the scientist, which would be in the form of a warning about which trails they would be able to travel with or without an escort. There had recently been a rash of animals in the jungle turning up injured, sick, and even diseased. Each member of the team took it upon himself to individually tour the research lab, so he would adapt to the facility equipment.

The next day the scientist were briefed on the specific areas of crime that each one of them would be expected to resolve. Only the President knew that there was one scientist among the twelve that had a premature formula already perfected. No one knew that there was a mad scientist on the same island who also was perfecting his own formula, this formula would give him the upper hand in crime sprees all around the world. This mad scientist name was Victor, and his plot was to use any means necessary to rule the world. Back at the laboratory, a brilliant scientist named, Gene, had begun working on a portion he thought would help save mankind from crime and destruction.

Gene was already ahead of the team, because he had this idea many years ago, and he was waiting for the right time to introduce his formula to the world. Gene knew the other scientist would want to know of his secret formula so he took it upon himself to hide it from his co-workers as if they had no knowledge of what he had already accomplished. Not knowing the side-effects of the formula, Gene waited till all the staff left the lab and took the formula back to his room, where he then took a shower and shaved. After a few hours had elapsed, Gene decided the best way to test his formula would, be to give it to the sick animals if possible without anyone knowing. Ah! The jungle would be the perfect place to test his formula and the subjects could only possibly grow stronger, increase in knowledge, and have a second chance at life. Gene packed himself a survivor backpack and pretend as if he were going to use the islanders as his escorts, but with the blink of an eye, he dotted off into the jungle where his research would continue for subjects on whom he would use his formula.

Gene finds himself deep into the dense jungle where he immediately comes in contact with an injured skunk. Equipped with his high tech glow head light, Gene shines a warm light onto the injured skunk. He slowly placed the pill into the skunk's mouth and all of a sudden the skunk begins to glow, bright colors rushed throughout its body, the skunk injuries began to heal and his body transformed into a hybrid creature of the night. Gene saw that his pill of wonder was an immediate success so he and the skunk traveled back through the dense jungle before anyone notice him missing. Gene placed the skunk in a secret compartment in his quarters located underneath the floorboard.

A week had pasted and the President placed a phone call to the laboratory to get an update on the progress of the secret 20 million- dollar experiment. Gene now knows that he has to work fast to complete the studies of his new subject in order to meet the critical needs of the president. Every night he performed test and log down information about the strengths and weakness of the skunk, that might aid him in his next creature of the Knight experiment.

Late into the evening, Gene would venture off into his secret compartment underneath his quarters, Gene's goal was to groom the skunk into some sort of avenger against crime, somewhat of a super crime fighter; better yet a superhero if you will. Meanwhile, Gene was proud of his success, Victor the mad scientist had also successfully created a formula that would turn any tame creature into a creature of terror, and mass destruction. The reason Victor was so hostile, was because he was abandon on the island many years ago by the order of the Science Commission, for performing evil covert operations of his own genius creations. One afternoon while performing laboratory experiments, one of the elite scientist mixed together an incorrect formula that created an explosion that rapidly spread poisonous fumes throughout the entire lab; therefore the smoke alarms begin ringing and the evacuation of the laboratory begin. All experiments and operations were temporarily halted until further notified by the project management. Gene now had plenty of time to complete his already advanced project while the other scientist enjoyed the Island Resorts. Almost immediately the president ordered the project to be abandoned, due to security leaks, until further noticed.

During the entire calamity, Gene prepared himself a backpack and journeyed back into the dense jungle in search of the remaining creatures for his continuing testing his formula. The skunk used his new senses to help locate Genes next subject and while completing the skunks training that would aid him in crime fighting, human adaptability, and fighting techniques. As the sun began to set, Gene and the skunk begin to set up camp along side the river, where all of a sudden Gene hears a noise, which he gave very little thought to an so he continued to place the heat sensors and silent alarms around the perimeter.

The bushes begin rattling once again and Gene didn't want to risk his project beginning discovered, so he told the skunk to take cover and wait until he revealed the source of the strange noise. Gene heard the noise once again, so he decided to set another trap and leave the area so whatever was creating this sound would hopefully trap it self. While setting the trap he noticed a broken branch; therefore he slowly scoured the area for evidence of another creature. Gene and the skunk noticed a lot of splashing among some Lilly pads, there they saw a toad with a limp leg leaping or attempting to leap from pad to pad. As Gene walked briskly beside the edge of the riverbank, the thought occurred to him that he could use his formula to treat the toad injuries. Tossing the capsule into the air allowing the toad to retrieve the capsule with its tongue from the air; thinking that the capsule was an insect. Once the toad swallowed the capsule, his body begins glowing, his injuries begin to heal and his body went into a metamorphous stage. Gene felt uncertain because he hadn't tried his experimental formula on an aquatic life form. Minutes later, the transformation was complete and Gene had one more subject to add to his fleet of Warriors. After successfully using several capsules, Gene feels that now his formula maybe successful, because the formula adapts to the creatures DNA.

Feeling confident he explains to the skunk and the toad why they were being selected and given a second chance. Once again the team resumes training the next morning and while jogging along the river bank, they hear sounds of howling near a wooded area in the nearby jungle, Gene immediately notice a dog like creature howling, because he was bound to an old ancient rusty trap. Gene and his team members carefully removed the wolf began to lash out from pure pain, so he had to tranquilized, which in turn allows Gene to place the capsule inside the wolf's mouth which took affect within minutes. Before the sun sets the wolf's body has totally healed and he is now capable of joining the rest of the team after being briefed on the secret project. The team members regroup and Gene retrieves all the equipment and they return back to base camp.

The wolf, toad, and the skunk gathered up fish and vegetables to eat for dinner. In the meanwhile everyone was eating and getting full, Gene explained that everyone should get plenty of rest because they would have a full day of traveling and training ahead of them tomorrow. The aroma from the leftovers ascended into the air attracting a raccoon, which gets a wit of the strong scent of stewed fish. The raccoon was suffering from malnutrition; therefore it was near its final stages before expiring. Suffering from hunger the raccoon uses its last bit of strength to tunnel underneath the sensors, only to find a very small portion of the stewed fish left in the bottom of the pot. This was just enough to give the raccoon energy to flee back into the woods, after being scared off by Gene, who had awaken from his brief moment of sleep to see a starving raccoon dangling from and empty pot, with hopes of only finding food.

As soon as day break came, Gene strolled into the outskirts of the woods, only to find the smart raccoon had tunneled underneath the sensor trap that he had set the day before. The raccoon lie near the trap in middle of transformation after eating small amount of stewed fish, which Gene had secretly placed a capsule before going to sleep. Gene, was quite aware of the starvation situation, so he knew sooner or later one of the creatures would be smart enough to defuse his trap. The raccoon and Gene returned to camp where he was briefed as the subjects were and he too accepted his faith and his new powers for the good of animals and mankind. The rest of the team greeted there new member and the rigorous training session continued.

The team jogged deep into the dense jungle only to stumble upon what they thought was a vacant cave, Gene suggested that the team stop for a break, and all of a sudden a pair of fiery yellow eyes appeared out of the dark and everyone scattered! Leaving Gene behind. Gene tried to calm the leopard, but the hungry leopard lunged toward Gene and he ran for the safety of a nearby tree, and at the same time the leopard ripped Genes pocket filled with the capsules. One quick swipe and the leopard thought he had and easy dinner. The leopard quickly eat several of the capsules, resulting in leaving the big cat unconscious for several hours. Gene helped toad, raccoon, and skunk to carry the leopard back toward the camp and he sent the wolf to scout the new trail ahead of them. The wolf did indeed come across a moving bush only to flush out a jackrabbit, which led the wolf into the feeding ground where the elephant and the rhinos were grazing. To Genes surprise these creatures volunteered to test the capsules that Gene had left over, for they had no fear of humans or fear from the creatures of the Knights. Gene tricked the jackrabbit to eat a carrot with the capsule planted inside and his body adapted as well as the other animals.

While in route back to the base camp the team of creatures ventured upon an injured hippo. The hippo had been severely wounded after battling with another hippo. The hippo lay helplessly on the edge of the riverbank about to take its last breath, until Gene slipped a capsule into the injured creature mouth. The hippo recovered and immediately joined the team of creatures, everyone remain at the riverbank campsite until the next day. Early the next morning everyone returned to the training trail only to be confronted by the loud sound of a hunter's rifle.

Gene glimpsed a blur tumbling from the sky at a great speed; several of the creatures scouted the distant area to locate whatever it was that had fallen from the sky. Behold! , The creatures located an injured eagle whose wing had been seriously wounded. As you would expect the eagle received treatment and was also recruited into the Creatures of the Knights. During the next few days, Gene recruited a porcupine, centipede, and so on. Gene told his Creatures of Knight that he must show his face to keep himself free of suspicion. Therefore, all of the creatures would have to remain in Gene's secret compartment until training has been complete and the secret project had been given the green light.

Gene perfected a tablet that would remove the desire for the creatures need to desire to hunt and harm one another. Little did Gene and the other scientist know that the mad scientist "Victor", was on the other side of the island and he had prepared his creatures for an attack on the entire planet. Victor randomly targeted many locations around the world to place each of his creatures of terror. The creatures begin to destroy and terrify and anyone and everything that tried to halt the mission that Victor had plotted. The President was immediately notified of the horror that had been unleashed upon the planet. The President contacted Gene at the laboratory on their hot line and issued the order to put the secret project into effect. Gene stepped forward and without hesitation unleashed the secret project at the Presidents request. How will the new guardians perform under the ever-watching eyes of the Mankind?

ZODIAC
KNIGHTS 2000
TM
LEO
TAURUS
It's Time!!!
SPECIAL Edition ★★★★★★ Potter Boys' Creation

ZODIAC KNIGHTS 2000
TM
LEO
TAURUS THE BULL
It's Time...!!!
SPECIAL Edition ****** Potter Boys' Creation

The Zodiac knights 2000, is a line of super-Hero action figures based upon a colony of fantasy characters that battle villians from Distant Planets in an attempt to save our planet.

These characters, name after the signs of the Zodiac, would have the combined features of an animal, Human, and machine. The zodiac knights bodies would consist of a muscular character with flexible wings extended from his shoulder blades, a Jet-pack strapped to his back, Jet-pack tubes running along the perimeter of his limbs, portable Mag-wheels built into his thighs, power boots, and power braces positioned at his forearms.

The symbol would be emblazoned on these warriors' chest and he would have a formidable appearance designed to exhibit power and strength against evil-doers. A "knight Transport" would serve as his means of Transportation between Galaxies.

GENE

Red
WOLF

SAMMY Skunck

RINO

Victor

ORANG - UTAN

OXEN

WALT

IBEX

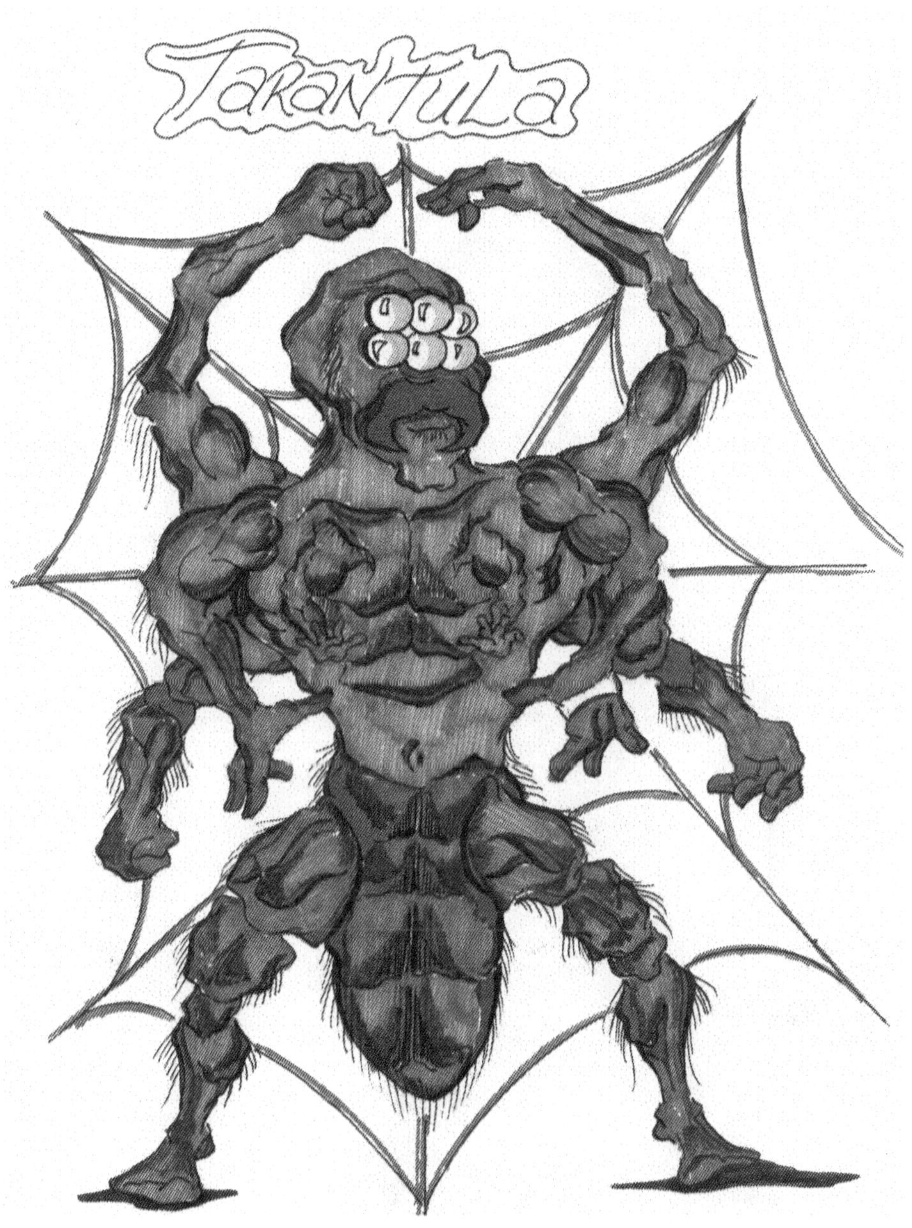

TARANTULA

Tuatara

The Shrine Warriors

Guardians of the Sacred Emblem

The year was 1700, in the land of Morocco. The Moroccans had absolute control and access to the entire Mediterranean Sea. The Moroccans were impatiently prepared to engage in battle with the Spanish soldiers. The Moroccans had received word that the Spaniards were preparing an elite unit of soldiers for war against Morocco inorder to seize power over all their land and resources. Jon Juan the commander and chief, ordered his elite unit to assemble and prepare to set sail for Spain into the deep lands of Morocco. Many hours had passed and Jon Juan and his elite unit was approaching the coastal waters of Morocco. The objective was to wait for the sun to set and allow the strong night winds and the moonlite undercurrents to bring them into the shore lines undetected. Soon night fall arrived and Jon Juan ordered his elite unit to advance upon the city and place explosives in the cracks of the Moroccan wall. After the wall came crashing down, the elite unit would move inside to blanket the city of Morocco with total precision.

To the surprise of the elite unit, the city was completely abandoned; this left the unit commander to believe that they were sitting in the middle of a preplanned ambush. This could only mean that there was a leak within the ranks of the elite unit or higher up command. Before Jon Juan could evacuate his soldiers from the city, a band of covert Moroccans pounced upon the unsuspecting soldiers. The small battle continued on for several hours, but the elite unit finally prevailed. Homes were destroyed and many soldiers were wounded in this brief battle for land and survival. The Moroccans were defeated therefore, they lost their land, power, and whatever resources they had aquired. Jon Juan stood towering upon the Moroccan's throne and claimed leadership over the Moroccan land and people . While sitting upon the throne and gazing into the sky thinking of his victory and how he would tailor the conquered city to fit a new ruler; Jon Juan forced the remainding refugees to began construction on his new palace even though they held hatred in their hearts for the conquering ruler.

There where five Moroccan bandits that had eluded the elite unit during the battle, at least they thought they had succeeded and planned to secretly dethrone the new ruler and take back their city.

Placing the commander out in the open for bait was a brillant plan to draw out any stray refugees that the unit hadn't captured. This was a tactical move by Jon Juan's elite unit to weed out any resistance within the city. The five Moroccans were immediately captured and placed within the walls of the mildewed, cold dark dungeon, which was used only for prisoners about to meet their death sentence in which whom had violated the law. The next day had finally arrived and Jon Juan would act as judge and jury, handing down the ultimate punishment for the refugee prisoners about to walk the thin line of survere punishment or a worse faith than death. Silence! Ordered Jon Juan to the on looking crowd, I am feeling very generous today and your judgement will be to leave the city of Morocco and never to return. The five Moroccans felt as if lady luck had shined upon them and they had cheated death by the skin of their teeth.

The elite soldiers escorted the five Moroccans to the palace gates, the soldiers warned that if there paths ever crossed again, that they would actually skin them alive and this would the best punishment they could hope for, before death. Even though the Moroccans thought that they were cheating death, Jon Juan knew very well of the torchure the desert could impose upon a man or men who weren't prepared to battle the terrible weather conditions that only the dessert could serve out to even the most wildeyed torment handed down from any man. The Moroccans began there journey at exactly the time the desert served it's hottest tempertures to any living breathing creature caught in its immense sunrays. If a soul survived the tremendous sunrays and lived to witness the freezing cold temperatures during the nights of the harsh desertenvironment, there would sure be very little hope of living to tell the tale to their next of kin. One of theMoroccans began to hallucinate, seeing images of cities and people that weren't there, the other Moroccan bandits cried out for water! I need water! All of the Moroccans began to develop blisters, bloodshoot eyes, and severely cracked dry skin as the desert punishment began to take it's toll on their weiry bodies.

This was the day that lady luck shined upon the five Moroccan bandits; by pure misdirection, the five bandits stumbbled upon a water hole where they as were able to capture some small game desert creatures to help ease the pain of starvation. Not even three hundred yards away barely still standing was the burnt ruins of an abandoned town, that was known as the town of "Tangier." The five Moroccans knew that they would have to use the burnt ruins as shelter from the deserts winds as night quickly approached.

This small town of Tangier, was also known to the conquering hands of Jon juan and his soldiers, which they had found to be only practice, because the rumor floating around was that the city of Morocco held a hidden treasure in which could escalate a man's power and wealth throughtout the world, only to be found in an object known as the Sacred Emblem. While inside of the town of ruins, the five bandits continued to search for food and rags to wear to shield them from the furious climate outside. Jon Juan had already known of the sacred emblems powers that it would crown the man or men who held it in his possession; it label him as the ultimate ruler of the world.

The refugees that were used to rebuild the city and the palace were beaten by the soldiers, inorder to reveal any information they had knowledge of or they had heard rumors about the sacred emblem. Many of the captives were punished within inches of their lives, only to leave Jon Juan with disappointing news, which anger him with his men. The fortune teller that he had brought with him, could only aid him if the treasures had been unearth, therefore she would be drawn to it's source of energy. Jon Juan announced to everyone that he would stop at nothing or any cost to posse the sacred emblem. The five Moroccans slept in the ruins knowing they would have to continue their travels as far away from the city of

Morocco as possible. They knew the soldiers would be sent to bring back the remainds of their bodies to satisfy Jon Juan's anger. The following morning one of the bandits stumbbled across a tavern that he thought might be a good place to maybe find some hidden food or clothing, but to his surprise! the tavern was and ancient burial ground for the towns hidden treasures for many centuries.

Screaming at the top of his lungs, and losing his voice all at the same time; within a matter of minutes he felt he would experience sure faint from the flying dust, he then sommoned the other four bandits to the secret passageway. After the other bandits rushed to the tavern with hast, hoping bad faith hadn't befallen their comrade. Everyone immediately forgot about all their pain and suffering and even Jon Juan, after seeing the eye-popping score of treasure that lined the burial ground walls.The eye couldn't see very far in the dustfilled, dark musty, tavern filled with spider webs and other creepy crawly creatures. As the bandits ventured further into the tavern, there were a variety of symbols etched into the walls along with the small embedded treasures. The tavern began to rummble, and a lot of debris fell from the upper part of the tavern, leaving a small opening for a dim view of sunlight to luminate what appeared to be the sacred emblem broken in to five medium size pieces. The bandits thought once again that their lives would end during all the trimmbling, only to standup still alive and shaking away the dust and dirt to see if they had been buried alive.

One of the bandits began to read the inscription on the walls and at the same time while trying to regain their sight, the five objects began to glow so bright that the bandits were blinded by the tremendous glow that illuminated the five objects. What the inscription didn't tell the bandits that whomever read from the inscription with a pure heart would become the guardians of the sacred emblem. This ment that the guardians would have to protect the sacred emblem form all evil-doers, including the likes of Jon Juan.

Mystical material all of a sudden emerge from the burial ground walls and wrapped the Moroccans until the mummification was complete. In a matter of hours the bandits were transformed into the guardians of the sacred emblem. Back in the fallen city of Morocco, Jon Juan's fortune teller begin receiving strong mystical viberations coming from the ruins of Tangier. Jon Juan was overwhelmed of the good news from his remaining favorite fortune teller and immediately deployed a scout unit to the area of the burnt ruins, only with instructions to report back with good news or not to report back at all!

Jon Juan issued the order to make sure that everything was destroyed and no one was alive departing with any hidden treasures. The desert owl would serve as a messenger if any sign of the sacred emblem was discovered. The five bandits awaken and realized that they had been choosen as the sacred guardians of the sacred emblem, their super senses alerted them that the first thing they had to do, was to split up and hide the sacred emblem pieces in different locations arouind the world. Each guardian would go into a long hibernation until all the sacred emblem pieces were recovered by the true of heart, no matter how long this would take, for these people would be trained and granted the true powers of the sacred emblem to protect the earth from all evil-doers. Upon arriving into the town of ruins the elite unit witnessed five intense glowing flying objects departing from within the ruins; they didn't know what to make of their ghostly discovery. The unit begin to search the burnt ruins finding nothing at first, but they knew they could not return without facing possible death if they returned without any news of finding the sacred emblem.

The commander shouted, we must find evidence or else everyone is sure to face the wrath of Jon Juan! Let's move to the next set of burnt ruins, stop! yelled one of the soldiers, I think I just might have found something of interest, Sir!. This had better be worth my time,the commander warned the soldier. Sir, there is a tavern that appears to have been hidden and it looks as if someone has been clearing a path futher inside.The commander sends in one team and awaits for them to send word that the tavern is clear and free of any dangerous conditions. The team discover the exact same burial ground walls embedded with small treasures and scrolled with an inscription. One of the soldiers begin to read from the inscription and the tavern started to rumble one again; except this time the soldiers removed a fraction of the treasure, which activated the wall to turn inside out and quicksand begun to fill the room. The walls sealed the team off from the other unit, but not before their cry for help was heard at the other end of the tavern, by the commander and team two. The soldiers were buried up to their necks in the ancient burial ground tavern with quicksand seemingly pouring from within the walls. The commander waited for the rumbling to stop and then he sent in a scout to set dynamite in the cracks of the walls, before his men were buried alive.

The scout immediately took whatever cover he could, because the explosives brought the stonewalls crumbling down. During the explosion, the debris blew all the way back to the entrance. At last team one could breath with relief, for they were free before they meet their doom. The commander reported back to Jon Juan their findings and he and another unit of his soldiers immediately headed in the direction of the town of tangier, with the fortune teller directing their path. The fortune teller told Jon Juan that the burnt ruins still held some viberation of mystical energy from the tavern underneath. Jon Juan told the fortune teller he was happy she was receiving the mystical energy from the ruins, but if he didn't unearth the sacred emblem, she had better use her nose like a bloodhound and locate the sacred emblem itself, or else!

Upon the arrival of Jon Juan, the commander ordered the soldiers to clear a path to be inspected by Jon Juan, this was done in a matter of minutes. Jon Juan gazed at the burial ground walls were a few ancient treasures remain evident. He immediately came across the impressions that held what appreared to have been the sacred emblem, which caused his face to fade into a deep shade of red with anger, he soon noticed the inscription and came to the conclusion that the five bandits had obtained the sacred emblem according to the inscription, this titled Jon Juan into a furious rage.

Jon Juan ordered the soldier to retrieve all the remaining artifacts and treasures and return immediately back to his new palace in Morocco. Months later, a farmer named Dewey, was having a very bad year with the harvest of his crops, which meant he had to find another way to feed his family. The winter would soon be arriving which left him with very few options to make up for a years worth of crop. Dewey left home in search of food for the winter months, crossing through the paths of the old Moroccan fields; He knew he was taking a chance with his life after Jon Juan had conquered the city of Morocco; it was immediately known to the people in the far countrysides, that if they were caught within the limits of the city, they would become Jon Juan's life time servants. Carefully walking along the side of a small creek, he decided to catch as many fish as possible and return home with the meat for the long winter months. Dewey caught a large amount of fish, soon after he begin gathering his belongs to head in the direction of home.

The sounds of soldiers marching and singing alerted him to take cover, he had to dive into the exact same creek he had caught his winter meal for his family. Dewey breath thru a hollow straw until the soldiers continued to march by, but wait a minute! a close call; one of the soldiers decided to fill his canteen with water from the fresh water creek. The soldier noticed a bubble or two surfacing and threw a couple of stones in the direction of the bubbles. The squad came to a halt, the unit leader turned and yelled to the soldier, that if he didn't return to the ranks, he would pull gurard duty for the rest of his life. While under the water, Dewey noticed a shiney metal object, he picked up the object and existed the creek to continue on his path back to the countryside of Morocco. He checked to see if the coast was clear, he could not afford to become a servant for Jon Juan and provide for his family too.

Dewey had become one of the first pure of heart to retrieve one of five pieces of the sacred emblem unknowningly; he could only admire the shiney object and wonder what was it's value and the history behind the precious metal object. The sun begin to set and Dewey knew he would become prey, instead of the hunter, walking thru the fields during the night. The nearest tall tree would serve as his haven from the Moroccan lions, who would pick up the sent of the fresh fish aroma sailing across the night air, like a dinner bell ringing. As luck would have it, the tree still had an old hunters rack perched high up in the tree for hunters who hunted in the wee hours at the break of dawn. Dewey knew he would have to risk his life by spending the entire night perched in the hunter's rack, high above the ground level. Sleeping in the hunter's rack would preserve his life so he could deliver the food the next day a sunrise. Dewey sat very still in the hunter's rack, where he heard bushes rattling and the roars of the large Moroccan lions, stirring in the fields below.

The roars of the lions grew closer and closer as the night winds carried the smell of fish into the brisk night breeze. Dewey knew he would have to sprinkle the fish with a special herb, so that the lions wouldn't hang around until the break of dawn. The lions where determined to scale the tree trunk to eat anything unleashing the ordor that smelled or resembled food. The special herbs smothered the immediate smell of fish long enough for the lions to catch the ordor of a fleeting deer. In a matter of minutes the lions had surrounded their prey and continued to feast on the deer carcass. Dewey made it through the night and woke up very earily the next morning, gathering all of his things and headed back in the direction of his home. As Dewey reaches the outskirts of Morocco, he witness Jon Juan soldiers unloading wagon loads of strange artifacts and placing them inside the palace valult. Taking a quick look at the fallen city , Dewey didn't think to much about the soldiers, the only thing on his mind at the moment he wanted get home safely to feed his family for the winter months.

Finally arriving safely with all his limbs still in tact, Dewey greeted his wife with several months supply of fresh trout, his wife stood in the doorway with eyes of tearful joy, for the winter months weren't very kind to man nor beast. In the meantime, Dewey sat in his chamber admiring his new shiney object that he knew very little about. The family sat down to eat dinner, Dewey told his wife he would have to go into to town to the ancient artifact shop to do some research on a new shiney object he found during his travels. Dewey made it into town without being captured by Jon Juan soldiers, where he arrived at the antique artifacts shopkeeper's location. He caustiously placed the shiney object in the hands of the shopkeeper, hoping that the artifact was of some value. Dewey asked the shopkeeper had he ever seen such a antique artifact with such a brillant glow? As the shopkeeper began to examine the object, Jon Juan and his soldiers arrived with urgent news of the ancient treasures that they had brought back. The shopkeeper was told to stop whatever he was doing and immediately examine several pieces of the treasure. It had been made mention that Jon Juan was seeking any object that had any relations with the well-known sacred emblem.

Without hesitation the shopkeeper placed Dewey's object to the side and examined the items Jon Juan had presented. Jon Juan did not realize how close he was to a piece of the sacred emblem. The shopkeeper trembled with fear and told Jon Juan that the ancient artifacts that he had discovered weren't part of the sacred emblem .Jon Juan warned the shopkeeper that if anyone comes into the shop with any parts of the sacred emblem, he had best notify him asap. Jon Juan and his soldiers vacated the shop, leaving

Dewey standing in the corner silently until the coast was clear. The shopkeeper reluctanly continued to observe Dewey's strange shiney metal object. Dewey asked the shopkeeper what was the strange object and did it have a history. The shopkeeper then reached down and pulled out a dusty old book on ancient artifacts, showing a wide range of sacred emblems form other times in history. To their surprise the object that Dewey presented resembled the exact same sacred emblem that Jon Juan had been threating every living soul about. The shopkeeper told Dewey that the special object held the spirit of the five Moroccan guardians, who are swornto protect the sacred emblem from all evil-doers.

After the shopkeeper told Dewey what he thought was good news to him;the shopkeeper grabbed the shiney object fom the sweaty hands of Dewey and ran toward the back door, only to be tackled by Dewey, who then took back his shiny object and hit the shopkeeper across his cranium, leaving him semiconscious.Dewey ran into the rear of the shop to hide. The shopkeeper dragged himself across the dirty wooden floor and pulled open the creeky rusty door, to yell for help. I found it! I found it! over here, Jon Juan and yelping about the object, because he didn't want Jon Juan to hold him true to his all but real threats. The hopkeeper said that the young man in the corner of my shop had possession of a piece of the sacred emblem that he had warned him to relay the urgent messeage. Jon Juan soldiers split into two teams and drew a sketch onto a scroll to be shown around, so that someone may collect the reward. Jon Juan ordered his soldiers to bring the young man and the sacred emblem back to his new palace unharmed, so he could lead him to the resting place of the remaining sacred emblem pieces.

Dewey knew he had to hide in the fields of Morocco, after fleeting the antique shop, inorder to elude Jon Juan soldiers. The soldiers knew that searching the fields would be like searching for a needle in a hay stack. The soldiers heard something moving in the bushes, only to be chased out of the fields by a wild boar that was feeding nearby. While the soldiers were fleeing, Dewey hurried back on his pathway to home. Dewey told his wife about the sacred emblem and he didn't have time to explain everything; but he knew he must protect the sacred emblem and keep it out of the evil hands of Jon Juan the tyrant ruler. Dewey packed a bag and told his wife he must take a trip to keep the family safe and out harms way from Jon Juan vengance. He kissed his wife and said I'll return when everthing settles down. There's enough food to feed the family until return. Dewey was off to discover Jon Juan's plan for the sacred emblem. Dewey came upon several ships docked that were being prepared for the voyage back to Asia. Dewey hide in the bush watching the workers loading the ships for their long journey. Many hours had pasted, the sun was setting and everything grew very quite around the peer. Dewey walked briskly on board an old fishing vessel, where he became a stowaway. The next morning the captain of the fishing vessel told the crew to raise the anchor, they were about to sail out to sea.

After several days Dewey's food supply began to run very low, so he knew he had to make a desparate attempt to mimic one of the hired ship hands; besides it would only be a matter of time before he would be discovered as a stowaway aboard a fishing vessel. The captain navigated the fishing vessel by the stars like they did in ancient times. The lookout sounded the bull horn to let the crew know that they were only hours away from docking in the shore lines of Asia. The crew lowered the anchor and continued to unload the fishing supplies. Dewey blended in with the rest of the crew and the captain said let's go down to the local beer parlor. Dewey returned to the ship while everyone was entertaining themselves before shipping out once again. As fast as he could, Dewey gathered all of his belongs and abandoned ship into the distant night, into this strange land known as Asia, without a clue, except to follow his instincts and explore the new land in hopes of finding another antique shop along the way. Dewey knew he had to remain in disguise to keep Jon Juan from discovering his secret identity as a shipmate, instead of a farmer.

Jon Juan once again relied on the advice of the fortune teller, help him apprehend the farmer and the sacred emblem as soon as possible. The fortune teller told Jon Juan that she was feeling the vibes of the mystical emblem moving farther and farther away; perhaps in the direction of the sea. Jon Juan ordered his soldiers to gather their equipment to began their journey across the coastal waters of Asia. Dewey traveled deeper into Asia in search of extra food and seeking more knowledge about the sacred emblem. Dewey knew he had to find a job to keep his disguise along with feeding and finding shelter for himself. Jon Juan and his soldiers had received a tip that a fishing vessel had left Morocco. The vessel that Jon Juan was using caught up with the fishing vessel and they searched the entire ship, because the fortune teller said that she felt strong vibes coming from the lower belly of the ship. Jon Juan became very angry and told the fortune teller that her services were coming very close to causing her pain and suffering, if his blood pressure continued to rise over her lack of success. Jon Juan reboarded his own vessel and ordered the captain to set sail for the Asian fishing ports. Hours had elasped and Jon Juan grew very impatient, he warned the captain to alert him as soon as the ship entiered the docks so he could immediately put the no good for an excuse of an fortune back to work and locate the farmer and his sacred emblem.

Dewey could smell the aroma being blown form afar that escaped from the ventalation of a sushi restaurant. The smell of food was so tempting, it cause his stomach to growl louder and louder. He trailed the aroma directly to the front door, where he asked timidly if they were hiring experienced sushi chef or even a dishwasher. Jon Juan's ship docked in the port, his soldiers unload all their supplies and visited the exact beer parlor that Dewey's shipmates had occupied earlier for drinks.Jon Juan entered the parlor and asked , if anyone had seen a stranger that resembled the man drawn on the scroll, this scroll as offered a handsome reward for the capture and safe return of the farmer and the sacred emblem. Dewey had no idea that Jon Juan had posted a reward for the capture and return of he and the sacred emblem; now a wanted man with a price on his head, Dewey knew he was not far enough away from the clutches of Jon Juan. The soldiers continued to carry on the search throughtout the city. The sushi house was about to close, when all of a sudden Jon Juan forced his small size six boot into the crack of the doorway before it closed for the night. Once inside, the soldiers began flashing a scroll and asking questions about the Moroccan farmer or any new strangers in town.

One of the local customers said that he thought that he might have seen the Moroccan farmer, but he was uncertain, his uncertainly got him thrown out on his head, for hendering progress. Sporting a new bruise on his forehead, the local told Jon Juan of the new dishwasher in the kitchen. Jon Juan told his soldiers to block the front and rear exist and entrances, so no one could ecscape an internal search of the restaurant and all the personnel and its patrons. While the local was confessing to Jon Juan, Dewey peaked through the kitchen door and saw that he was trapped inside by the soldiers. Dewey scampered around looking for a way out, so he climbed up into the ceiling of the kitchen and hide in the ceiling , holding his breath until it was safe to escape through a nearby window. Jon Juan ordered his soldiers to move in and search the kitchen, but to no avail, they had been outwitted once again. Where is he?looking directly at the fortune teller with his eyes begining to chris-cross with rage. Find him immediately! and bring him to me unharmed. The soldiers split into two teams and continued to scour the city once again.

As the sun begin to set, Dewey saw an oppurtunity to escape out of the kitchen window, without being seen. Dewey could hear the sounds of a roaring engine. The sounds of the engine got closer and closer and so did

Jon Juan soldiers. Dewey knew he would have to run for the engine, because he knew now that he had a bounty on his head and the sacred emblem. The roaring engine came through at a high rate of speed, Dewey knew he couldn't out run Jon Juan soldiers on foot, so he did what came natural and that was to run for the roaring engine. Jon Juan soldiers were hot on his trail and this could spell the end for Dewey , with just one slip and fall. The box cars continued to roar past Dewey, the soldiers were about to apprehend Dewey, as the kaboose was about to pass him by. Dewey leaped on to the train only inches away from the soldiers grasping fingers, which were about to capture him in a matter of seconds.Jon Juan soldiers returned with disappointing news that Dewey had escaped from them by leaping onto the train. Boiling in a furious rage, Jon Juan had all the soldiers shaved completely bald to ease his bloodpressure.

Jon Juan ordered the soldiers to continue to pursue the next train, heading in the same direction that the farmer and his sacred emblem were headed. Dewey didn't know exactly where the train was destined for, as long as he wasn't captured by Jon Juan and his soldiers. The train came to an abrut stop, Dewey's ride had come to an end. Frantically looking around, the train appear to be empty. Dewey caustionusly got off the train not knowing anything about the new city he is now about to embark upon. Dewey wondered into a town where everyone was on the street selling merchandise. Dewey walked past a merchant's shop, where he asked the merchant what is the name of your city? The merchant replied your in China. Dewey thought to himself, I'm a long ways from home. Walking futher thru the marketplace, where he came upon a merchant who buys and sells ancient artifacts. Dewey told the merchant he had an old artifact and could he tell him of it's history and value.The merchant was stunned to see such a rare ancient artifact.

While appraising the ancient artificact, there where two men in black robes that entered the antique shop with an ora of evil energy surrounding them. The two men in black robes where there to give Hang-loa a message, and at the same time Hang-loa hide the sacred emblem while conversating with the robed men in black. The robed men told Hang-loa that he had twenty-four hours to pay back the money he borrowed to open his antique shop. Hang-loa didn't have a clue where he would come up with a million zenny in currency. Hang-loa asked Dewey to come with him to his uncle's shop, he could tell us more about your ancient artifact.The two black robed men continued to walk the mean streets of China town making their weekly collections. Hang-loa and Dewey were walking toward the sushi restaurant, all of a sudden they heard a loud scream coming form a nearby alley. Dewey and Hang-loa rushed toward the alley only to find that there was no trace of a victim in need of help to be found. Hang-loa and Dewey looked at each other as if they were both half crazy. The two men started back in the direction of the restaurant, when for a breif moment they thought they heard another sound from behind the dumpster, in the spooky alley. Dewey told Hang-loa, since this was his neighbor he should be the one to take a look behind the dumpster. Hang-loa stood with a blank look on his face, he had located another piece that belong to the sacred emblem as well.

Hang-loa did not know that he was about to become a new member of the elite group of guardians.Hang-loa immediately picked up the artifact, and told Dewey we'll take the artifacts to my uncle's shop, he'll know exactly what these strange artifacts represent or where they originated from. Hang-loa and Dewey forgot all about eating dinner so they rushed over to his uncle's antique shop for his professonial opinion. The young men eagerly approached his uncle Wang-chow's antique shop, we are now closed sign was already hanging in the window. Hang-loa told Dewey let's go to my house and we'll return early in the morning, at first light, when the shop is open for business. Late into the evening, Hang-lo prepared dinner for his guest Dewey. Dewey didn't get a good nights sleep, because his unconcious mind gave him night mares about being captured by the notorious Jon Juan.

The rooster crowed and woke up the entire community, Hang-loa told Dewey that they should hurry and get dressed before the customers fill the store to purchase rare artifacts. The fortune teller told Jon Juan that the vibe was very strong in the direction of China. Jon Juan and his soldiers finally arrived in the city of China. A cold chill came over Dewey, as if the spirit of Jon Juan was hanging over his shoulder.

The elite unit of soldiers continued to search the train and every merchants antique shop, asking everyone had they seen any new strangers fitting the picture on the scroll. An elderly man told Jon Juan he had seen the farmer that he might be looking for walking with another antique merchant's nephew. The shop could be found on the outskirts of town. The fortune teller could not verify this information, because she still had a headache from the last tongue lashing that Jon Juan had thrusted upon her fragile senses. Jon Juan told the soldiers that they were going to follow his gut feeling this time, and maybe the fortune teller could recharge her scrammbled channels. Hang-loa told Dewey,"my uncle will have very good news for you and I ."Trouble was also on it's way to Hang-loa uncle's antique shop. Good morning uncle!, Ah, Hang-loa is that you, it's nice to see you in good health today. This is my friend Dewey, we brought some old ancient artifacts for you to examine. Where are they? Let me see them, Ah!

these are some very rare pieces of ancient artifacts. These artifacts that you have here are very priceless.

Come, I'll show you what these old ancient artifacts represent and there history and the meaning behind them. While in the back of the antique shop, Jon Juan and his soldiers were escorted by the men in the black robes. Jon Juan abruptly entered the antique shop. Ring!Ring!Ring! yes, yes how may I help you today. Jon Juan showed the merchant a scroll picture of a farmer, have you seen this man? Hang-loa and Dewey voices as they walked closer to the curtain, they heard the voices of the robed men questioning his uncle about the farmer and the young merchant. Jon Juan insist that the merchant allow his soldiers to search his antique shop with no delay. The merchant spoke very loudly to hint to Hang-loa and Dewey, so they could slip out through a hidden passage his uncle told him about in case of an emergency. Jon Juan became very impatient with the old merchant and told his soldiers to leave no spot unturned, until he was satisfied. The men in black robes asked once again, do you know where the farmer and the young merchant are? The old man answered no. One of the soldiers told Jon Juan he had found a passage, they must have escaped through here.

We'll deal with the old man later, said Jon Juan as he passed closely by the old man and stomped on his corned feet. The old men yelled out in pain immediately grabbing his foot. The soldiers begin closing the store at once, and the two men in black robes searched the corridor where they found a piece of Dewey's clothing in the wooden frame of the corridor.Hang-loa had used his uncle's corridor before, he told Dewey it would lead directly to the harbor. Hang-loa and Dewey existed the corridor were they came upon an old sea captain, who just so happen to be looking for some good fishing hands. Hang-loa and Dewey knew if they didn't take the job they would be captured by Jon Juan soldiers. Moments away from capture, Hang-loa and Dewey set sail with the sea captain. Jon Juan and his soldiers apprehended another sea vessel to pursue the departing vessel. Jon Juan was delayed because the ship they took was under repairs, which slowed their progress. Hang-loa and Dewey wanted to know where they were going, so they asked the sea captain, where are we headed? The sea captain replied "Alaska, where fish are plentiful." The sea captain told Hang-loa and Dewey to put on the suites below, it would be a a long cold journey ahead of us.

The sea captain continue to sail ahead and the sun begin to set and the night air got colder. The old sea captain told Hang-loa and Dewey to keep the hopper filled with coals if they didn't want to become human posicles, while manning the ship. The fog grew thicker and thicker and the sea captain couldn't see two feet in front of himself. This was the receipe for a bad strom. When the fog finally cleared, the ship had barely missed an iceberg off the starboard bow. The captain told Hang-loa and Dewey to hang on were're going to make a sharp turn. The old captain turned the vessel as hard as he could but, the iceberg scaved the side of the ship, damaging a small amount of the outer hull. Hang-loa and Dewey both took a deep breath and asked the captain was this a normal outting. The captain replied "all my years of sailing I've never hit an iceburg, what did it do to the side of the ship? It damaged the outer hull, lucky for us we're only a few miles from the Alaska coastline.

Finally making it to the Alaskan coastline, the sea captain told Hang-loa and Dewey to unload the fishing equipment, so they could get out of the bad storm, and have an early start fishing tommorow. Hang-loa told Dewey they could take a break and warm themselves by a nearby barrel of fire next to the cabin where it's nice and warm. Mean while, back in China, Jon Juan and his men abandoned the damaged ship and chartered another ship to sail in search of the wanted men and the ancient artifacts that Jon Juan so desperately desired. Back in Alaska, Hang-loa and Dewey begin to discuss their next plan to elude Jon Juan and find a resting place for the ancient artifacts. The sea captain returned and brought the two men some hot chocolate and a piece of beef jerky, out of the blue the sea captain began to telling old fishing stories that he had experienced when he was a young lad. As time pasted, the sea captain said well that enough about me, you men are going to need all your rest and strength for the big day tommorow, as soon as this storm dies down.

Morning came soon, the old sea captain brought out the insulated suites for Hang-loa and Dewey to wear for enduring the severe weather. Hang-loa and Dewey were awaken by the aroma of breakfast cooking in the galley. The sea captain told Hang-loa and Dewey to suite up, they would be leaving for the sea shortly. come, let's eat we have a long day ahead of us men. Back in China, Jon Juan and his men set sail for Alaska where Hang-loa and Dewey were headed out to sea on a fishing vessel. Jon Juan ask the captain how long would it take to get to the Alaskan shores, the captain told Jon Juan, depending on the weather, it could be a week or more. Jon Juan said to the captain besure we get to Alaska as soon as possible or else. He would not lose his treasure again due to foul ups. The old sea captain told Hang-loa and Dewey that breakfast is now over, let's go and repair the holes on the side of the ships hull that nearly was ripped away by the iceberg. We'll men grab your tools, let's get to work, there is no time to waste, Dewey and

Hang-loa agreed knowing that Jon Juan was hot on their trail with a bounty on their heads and the sacred emblem. These men knew they couldn't rest until lthe emblems were returned to their sacred burial grounds as one unit. Will Jon Juan eventually capture Dewey and Hang-loa.

Will the two young men successfully retrieve all the pieces to the sacred emblem and lay it to rest once and for all from all evil-doers and their evil intentions.

ZODIAC KNIGHTS 2000
TM
LEO
TAURUS the Bull.
It's Time.!!!
SPECIAL Edition ****** Potter Boys' Creation

Jon Juan
Tyrant Ruler

Isaac A. Potter Jr.

Ivan

Pierce the Spy

Mike the MINER

Black Robed Men
Tax Collectors

HANG-LOA MERCHANT

Elite Soliders

DEWEY
THE FARMER

"Zodiac Knights 2000"

GENERAL CONSIDERATIONS

This Information Summary relates to a product Line called "ZODIAC KNIGHTS 2000" which has been disclosed by Mr. Isaac A. Potter Jr., and Samuel J. Potter, of Monroe Louisiana. This Information Summary is based upon information and disclosure submitted by the originator along with notes from conversations with sales representatives. We have also supplied general marketing information tailored to "ZODIAC KNIGHTS 2000" and have made suggestions when appropriate. The result is a reference tool which can be used to submit "ZODIAC KNIGHTS 2000" to industry in a logical format which stresses its positive and most appealing features.

In preparing the Basic Information Package, we utilize standard statistical data with a heavy orientation on material prepared by the U.S. Department of Commerce and the Bureau of the Census. We attempt to supplement this data with more specialized information available from other basic marketing reference works, trade associations, trade publications, libraries, and other sources. The statistics provided in this report should not be interpreted as projections. Statistics generally lag two or more years behind the currrent year because of the time required by the various sources to compile and summerize the figures.

DESCRIPTION: Product Concept Review

In this Information Summary, we will review the distinctive features of the product line and the needs it may fulfill. The concept of the "ZODIAC KNIGHTS 2000", is a line of super-hero, action figures based upon a colony of fantasy characters that battle villians from distant planets in an attempt to save our planet. These characters, named after the signs of the Zodiac, would have the combined features of an animal, human, and machine. Pisces, for example, would consist of a muscular character with flexible wings extended from his jet pack, a jet pack strapped to his back, jet pack tubes running along the perimeter of his limbs, portable mag-wheels built into his thighs, power boots, and power braces positioned at his forearms. The symbol of Pisces would be emblazoned on this warrior's chest and he would have a formidable appearance designed to exhibit power and strength against evil-doers. A "Knight Transport" would serve as his means of transportation between galaxies.

GENERAL CONSIDERATIONS

If manufactured, this product line could contain individual dolls approximately 7 inches tall and constucted from molded plastic or rubber, The "ZODIAC KNIGHTS 2000" characters could be produced with colorful body components and accessories to add to their visual appeal. These super-hero dolls would provide a child with a toy that would challenge his imagination and foster creative playtime.

Function and Appealing Features

"ZODIAC KNIGHTS 2000" are being suggested, because we believe they would fulfill the need for a line of super-hero action figures designed to encourage a child to use his imagation. The appealing features of "ZODIAC KNIGHTS 2000" would be the diverse product line that would consist of a variety of characters named for each sign of the zodiac. These interestingly designed action figures would allow a child to use his imagination to create make-believe stories and scenarios involving the "ZODIAC KNIGHTS 2000". These dolls could be sold as individual units or in sets containing varying numbers of figures. A child may enjoy building a collection of these dolls until a complete set has been formed.

These action figures could be produced from molded plastic or rubber and jointed so that their body parts could be easily moved for posing them in a variety of ways.

GENERAL CONSIDERATIONS

Historical Development

The Potter Boys Creations Inc., identified a need or a problem to be solved that prompted him into the invention process. They then conceived "ZODIAC KNIGHTS 2000". Subsequently, sketches/drawings and a written description were prepared to manufacture or market "ZODIAC KNIGHTS 2000".

PRODUCTION CONSIDERATION

Feasibility

One of the initial steps in presenting a new concept to industry is deterining its feasibility. The work is based on the premise that the originator has predetermined that "ZODIAC KNIGHTS 2000" will work, function as designed, serve the intended purpose, and accomplish those objectives desired. We do not express an opinion regarding feasibility nor do we make projections regarding the success of an idea or concept as the elements involved in marketing are many and complex.

Producibility

It appears that "ZODIAC KNIGHTS 2000" could be produced easily using conventional and readily available materials and manufacturing processes. No new production technology would be required. "ZODIAC KNIGHTS 2000" could be produced from a plastic such as polyethylene. This material, which is readily available in a variety of colors, is reasonably priced and easily formed by a wide range of plastic processors. Injection molded might be a standard approach to production. The character's facial features could be hand-painted or machine imprinted during manufacture.

PRODUCTION CONSIDERATIONS

Packaging

Isaac A. Potter Jr.

In the event "ZODIAC KNIGHTS 2000" are manufactured, they will require a package. Manufacturers and marketers are becoming increasingly aware of the importance of product packaging in developing consumer recognition. Developing a package for a new product involves numerous considerations. Some packaging concerns include protection, economy, convenience, promotion, and ecology. The first task is to establish a packaging concept, or a definition of what the package should basically be or do for the particular product. Also, the manufactuer must make decisions regarding the component elements of package design, such as size, shape, materials, color, text and brand mark. The packaging elements must also be guided by decisions on pricing, advertising, and other marketing elements. Perhaps the most important packaging concern is convenience to the consumer. For a product package to be convenient to consumers, it should be easy to open. With the rise in consumer affluence, consumers are willing to pay a little more for the convenience, appearance, dependability, and prestige of better packaging.

After package is designed, it should be subjected to engineering test to ensure that it will stand up under normal conditions, visual tests to ensure that the text is legible and the colors harmonious, dealer tests to ensure that dealers find the package attractive and easy to handle, and consumer tests to determine favorable or unfavorable responses.

PRODUCTION CONSIDERATIONS

In this section, we will make a suggestion regarding the physical package for "ZODIAC KNIGHTS 2000". Later in this report under the PROMOTIONAL CONDERATIONS section, we will review the promotional aspects of product packaging. "ZODIAC KNIGHTS 2000" could be packaged in a cardboard pressboard box, sized to the product. The package could have a viewing window for product visibility. The package could have a label printed in one or more colors (including four-color process) on a pressure-sensitive paper stock. Ideally, the label would not only identify the product but also show it in use. Corrugated cardboard shipping containers would then be used to hold a quantity of individually packaged products to facilitate shipment and storage.

Cost Estimates

A wide range of factors influence the selling price, distribution channel markups, and unit cost of a product. The large number of variables and their fluctuations make it exceedingly difficult (if not impossible) to accurately estimate price, markups, and cost factors short of actual manufacture and distribution. One common approach towards the selection of a possible selling price considers "positioning" of the proposed product relative to other existing products with similar attributes. Price positioning therefore is part of the overall market position and reflects a price which could be in line with the potential perceived value for the proposed product. Once "price" or "perceived value" is estimated, consideration can then be given to what type of markup structure could reasonably be used to arrive at such a final selling price, given known or estimated markup correlations between retailers, wholesalers or distributors, and manufacturers. We use a retrospective approach and work with an estimated selling price to approiximate wholesaler markups and manufacturing cost. Manufacturers, in determining their prices, also consider such factors as fixed costs associated with plant, equipment , and tooling; factors such as the costs of raw materials, labor (affected by automation), assembly techniques, packaging, and overhead; and marketing variables such as costs of shipping and handling, sales expenses, warranty and return factors, factor of loss, overhead, competitive pricing, geographic and demographic location, etc.

Within the scope of this Basic Information Package report, even the best efforts can result in deriving only rough approximations for the positioning of selling price, corresponding distributor channel markups, and potential of selling price, corresponding distributor channel markups, and potential manuifacturing cost. For working purposes in preparing this Information Summary, howerver, we project an estimated pricing structure as follows:

Manufacturing Cost:

Wholsale Price:

Retail Price:

MARKETING CONSIDERATIONS

Competitive Environment

When considering the introduction of the new product to the marketplace, one of the factors that should be considered is the competitive environment. Efforts should be made to learn what existing competitors are offering to their customers and the customers' wants and needs. A new product introduction can be an improved or modified version of an existing product or it can be a totally new product innovation. In either case, the competitive environment should be studied to determine the existence of similar or identical products. The Potters' have disclosed a belief that this product concept is original concept. We conduct a necessarily limited check of the marketplace for competitive products. An in-depth investigation is not possible as there is no definite way to assure that an idea or product has not been tried or thought of in the past or is not now in use somewhere in our country or elsewhere. In addition, the comptitive environment changes daily,. Old products disappear; new one appear. Seasonal trends also influence the availability of products. While a check of the marketplace may turn up nothing today, a similar product may even be on the drawing board in preparation of actual manufacture, and of course there would be no way for us to know of its existence. Acompetitive product may also be available within a specific geographical market area or available only on a limited basis as part of a test marketing program.

MARKETING CONSIDERATIONS

Benefits, Appeals, and Trends

Many factors influence the acceptance of a product in the marketplace. Two of the major factors relate to the needs a product fulfills (the benefits) and a desire to own that product (the appeal and /or a combination of these factors.) Also important are the trends and outlook of the industry pertaining to the invention. Within this section of our Information Summary, we will consider the various benefits, appeals, and trends which relates to "ZODIAC KNIGHTS 2000". The Potter Boys suggested the manufacture of a line of action figures that would be based upon a storylineof a race of warriors whose goal is to battle evil villains in a continued effort to save our planet. The "ZODIAC KNIGHTS 2000" would have an interesting physical composition. Each warrior would have the combined features of a human, animal, and machine. Their muscular bodies would be enhanced with integrated, powerful mags; jet packs; and braces. Each "ZODIAC KNIGHTS 2000" warrior would bear the zodiac symbol after which he would be named on his breast.

MARKETING CONSIDERATIONS

Children, particularly boys, may find these interestingly designed characters entertaining to play with because of their unusual appearance, poseable body components, and their potential to stimulate his imagination.

Isaac A. Potter Jr.

A child could create a variety of storylines in which the "ZODIAC KNIGHTS 2000" could wage battles against their evil counterparts. A child could enjoy hours of creative playtime with these knights and may desire to collect them until he has a complete set. In addition to battling evil, The Potters has suggested that these characters could be used in a campaign to educate children about overcoming negative obstacles that may be in their lives. They believe that a major benefit that could be derived from the "ZODIAC KNIGHTS 2000" figures would be that it would take an individual's mind off cruelty or unpleasant circumstances in the world around him. The "ZODIAC KNIGHTS 2000" could be used to act out aggression against situations that anger an individual and, therefore, provide him with a healthy outlet for venting negative feelings.

MARKETING CONSIDERATIONS

In addition, the legend continues with He-Man—-good versus evil. Young boys love classical male action archetypes as he squares off against his arch enemy, Skeletor. For those who like the extra macho type, the new Thunder Punch He-Man will be twice as impressive as he squares off with the gruesome Battle Blade Skeletor, his adversary, with glow-in- the -dark skull armor on his chest and an alarming blade-throwing feature. The introduction of such action figures for the 2003 Holiday buying season bodes well for products such as the "ZODIAC KNIGHTS 2000". It could indicate a beginning of a trend away from video games toward more basic toys that challenge a child's creativity and imagination. Since this product line would most probably be manufactured by the toy industry, it is important to note the conditions of and trends applicable to this industry. Generally speaking, the potential sales for any given toy or game is a figure that cannot be predicted with great certainty. Success in the toy industry involves capturing the whims of children and assessing intangibles such as "play value." Good decisions seem more a product of intution that of modern management techniques, but intuitive choices bear high risk. The "Cabbage Patch" dolls, for example, were reportedly turned down by five toy companies before Coleco saw their potential. Expanding successful product lines, using more extensive marketing research, relying more on licensing, and adopting more sophisticated advertising techniques have reduced risks to some extent.

MARKETING CONSIDERATIONS

Recent marketing strategies used by the major U.S. toy makers have been the linking of toys to popular cartoons or comic books and the adoption of fantasy storylines. This is especially true in the category of action figures, such a Mattel's "He-Man" and the other "Masters of the Universe" characters. In fact, Mattel recently reintroduced the "He Man", complete with a new space-fantasy theme, after deeming it premature to have withdrawn it from the market. A better example is the far-fetched premise of the "Teenage Mutant Ninja Turtles" —- adolescent reptilian victims of radioactive goo named after famous artists, living in the sewers of New York, pizza and practing martial arts, there are others, the Power Rangers, Poke Mon, Digi Mon, Spiderman etc. It is fantastic themes like these that are capturing the imaginations of the nation's children and selling action figures.

One of the most important factors to consider in the new product development process is the size of the potential market. For the purposes of this report, a "market" is defined as the "set of potential purchasers" of a new product. While few products have universal appeal, it is possible to generally define a broad market to give an indication of its size. Since most products are targeted to specific groups of consumers with specialized interests, it is often possible to segment the market into submarkets. Each submarket differs in its requirements, buying habits, or other critical characteristics. It is not our intention in this section to imply that all or even any of the markets identified would represent actual purchasers of "ZODIAC KNIGHTS 2000". Our purpose is simply to identify those groups which we view as being appropriate potential market targets for the invention in the event that it is manufactured and marketed. The Primary Market would consist of the parents of elementary school-aged boys who are about age 6 through 12.

Distribution Channels

Once the potential market targets for a new product have been identified, consideration should be given to identifying the types of outlets where the product could potentially be distributed to those market targets. In this section, we will identify potential channels of distribution for "ZODIAC KNIGHT 2000". However, there is absolutely no way that anyone can project with any accuracy the number of distribution outlets which might actually handle any give product. In obtaining the number of out lets for a particular distribution channel, we utilize information provided in the U.S. geographic area series of the Census of Retail Trade, Census of Wholesale Trade, and the Bureau of the Census, we rely upon business lists. The following channels represent potential outlets where "ZODIAC KNIGHTS 2000" could be distributed:

Conventional Department Stores

Discount or Mass Merchandising

Department Stores

National Chain Department Stores

Toy, Game, and Hobby Stores

Variety Stores

Gift Stores

Novelty Stores

Souvenir Stores

Wholesalers of Toys and Hobby Goods

Distribution to the International market would involve selected exporters as indicated below:

Exporters of Toys, Amusement, Sporting, and Athletic Goods:

Wholesale Exporters of Sporting, Reactions, Photographic and Hobby Goods, Toys, and Supplies

About the Author

Isaac A. Potter Jr., is a veteran, having served in the United States Army, freelance graphic,writer illustrator, and most of all a father to five beautiful children, a full time job. Isaac Potter grew up in a town called Monroe, Louisiana attended high school(Wossman High), Robinson Business College and Florida Metropolitian University in the state of Orlando,Florida. Samuel Potter is a father of three lovely children and is a mechanic, writer and a jack of all trades as is all the brothers including Patrick Potter Known in our small town as the " Potter Boys".

Reared in a smaller town known as Richwood Louisiana, life was aways one adventure after another growing up in the country setting teaming with cotton fields, fish and game also known as the Sportsman Paradise.

The Potter Boy's goal is to elevate to themselves to the Next Level and take their readers to a place where they can embrace their mental as well as their physical time.